LOKI AND SIGYN:

A LOVE STORY

YOUNG GODS IN LOVE

J. L. BUTLER

INTRODUCTION

This is the retelling of the old Norse legend of Loki, the god of Mischief, and his wife Sigyn. In the original legend Loki was the most intelligent and most attractive of all the Viking gods. His quick wit and penchant for playing practical jokes on his fellow Aesir (Norse gods) often got him into trouble. His intelligence and ability to think fast almost always got him out of it.

In the end, legend says that Loki crashed a party of all the gods. At this party, Loki revealed all the dirty little secrets of the gods and finally over stepped his bounds. The gods captured him and brought his sons Narfi and Vali to him. They turned Vali into a wolf that killed his brother, Narfi. The gods then took the entrails of Loki's son and used them as a rope to tie him to three rocks. A snake protruded above his head from the rocks. The snake was to drip poison onto Loki's face until Ragnarok (the Viking equivalent to Armageddon).

Loki's loyal wife Sigyn volunteered to stay with her husband, holding a bowl between Loki and the snake so that she could catch the poison and give Loki relief.

In my research of Loki and the old Norse gods and goddesses, it seemed that Loki was an unfairly maligned character. Sigyn's devotion to Loki seemed to indicate a great love story existed somewhere in Loki's past. I wondered, what was it like to have been born a god? What would it have been like to have grown up in Asgard, the home of the gods? What if Loki and Sigyn had grown up together and been childhood sweethearts? And finally, what if Odin had gotten it all wrong, and Loki didn't have to be the architect of Ragnarok?

I felt Loki and Sigyn and their sons deserved a better ending, and this little book is my attempt to give it to them.

Enjoy, and may the Chaos be with you!

Dedicated to my very good friend Ed McDaniel, whose wit and wisdom proved invaluable, and to my very good friend Dayna Tirado, whose encouragement and belief in me kept me going.

Special thanks to my friend Maggie Duncan, whose Proofreading and advice are priceless.

*Also, **very** special thanks to my daughter Beth, my best creation ever, and to her extraordinary son, Tommy, and loving husband, Chris, all of whom I love more than words can say.*

They once were children. Playfully competitive, they would tease and wrestle one another like any brothers, anywhere. Thor excelled at all things physically challenging; his brother, Loki, at things more intellectual and metaphysical. Thor, even as a young child, was heavier and stronger than Loki; Loki, a bit younger, was built more like a sprinter – wiry and agile, like a cat. Odin seemed to favor his elder son. He would often take Thor with him on hunting trips, while Loki stayed behind, with his mother and his tutor, Syr. Syr was in fact a practitioner of magic. She loved her bright little student, Loki, and taught him harmless tricks such as levitation and movement of small objects, like tableware and cups.

The children marked their birthdays according to the calendar of Midgard, or the sister Realm of Midgard, also known as Earth.

They aged much more slowly than Earth's native inhabitants. They were in fact hundreds of years old measured in Earth years while appearing only ten or twelve in Asgard.

One day, a new student entered the classroom of Thor, Loki, and Syr. A young girl, the same age as Loki, came to learn from Syr. She was a distant cousin of Odin, and had shown some mystical abilities herself. Her magic was bound to her voice; she could bend anyone to her will by simply singing a little song, telling them what she wanted. Her influence seemed to affect only those outside of the royal family – her sweet voice had no effect on either Thor or Loki, though Loki would often ask her to try and then gaze dreamily at her as she sang verse after ineffectual verse, only to finally stop, being quite vexed with him, indeed.

This was Sigyn, a native of Vanaheim, one of the sister realms of Asgard. Sigyn's father, Arngeirr, was a distant cousin to King Odin. Odin's wife, Frigga, generously offered.

for Sigyn to be tutored along with her sons, hoping that her influence might tame the rowdy young boys. Thor seemed quite bored with her and all things he considered girlish, but Loki was very taken with her. She seemed only tolerant of him, but the two soon became inseparable.

Unbeknownst to the children, these were in fact dark days for Asgard. Fingardin, a half-mortal, who controlled a large and powerful realm on the planet

Earth, had formed a loose alliance with the Frost Giants of Jotunheim. The Frost Giants were no friends to Odin and Asgard and had been held in check only because the two realms were very equally matched. Fingardin's powers were quite weak, but what he lacked in magical power was made up for in heavy metal. He had accumulated an enormous arsenal of Elven weapons, mostly acquired through the trade of human slaves to work the Elven mines and factories. Odin wished to keep his potential enemy, Fingardin, close. He orchestrated a great feast to celebrate Fingardin's 300th birthday. For an immortal, 300 years was not old at all, but Fingardin was half mortal and beginning to show his age.

Fingardin arrived at the gates of Asgard with an entourage of 500 of his "closest friends." He and his half-blood friends were brutes; their wretched smell—body order, dead meat, and ale--preceded them by a mile. They were loud and ill-mannered and showed a complete disrespect towards their host and hostess. During the brief, three-day course of their stay, dozens of serving girls were raped, and at least three Asgardians were found beaten to death in alleyways. It was all Odin could do to keep his men (and himself) from slaughtering these disgusting pig-men. He had to constantly remind himself that he had to remain friendly with Fingardin and his weapon-laden realm if he were to avoid a war with Jotunheim.

As Fingardin was burping and farting his farewells to Odin, he spotted the maiden Sigyn. Though still a young girl, Sigyn showed every sign of becoming a great beauty.

"And who owns that little wench?" he asked Odin.

"We have no slaves here, Fingardin. That girl is my cousin Arngeirr's only child, Sigyn. She is here in Asgard to study with my sons Thor and Loki." Odin despised this man, watching as actual drool rolled from the corner of his mouth as he leered at the little girl.

"Your cousin, eh? Then as a member of the royal family of Odin, if she were to wed, say, a member of the royal family of Fingardin, then the two families would be bound in fealty forever, wouldn't they?" An evil smile crept across the hideous old man's face.

Odin tried to hide his disgust. "A girl so young may not wed in this realm, Fingardin, even with parental consent. This royal family member you speak of should look elsewhere for a bride, I think."

Fingardin's face darkened. "Of course, of course, but she may wed as soon as she enters womanhood in these parts, may she not? With parental permission, I mean." He knotted his hands together, continuing to stare at the girl. "And what father wouldn't give up one child for the sake of the safety of millions?" The sly grin was back.

Odin's heart sank. He couldn't imagine condemning any poor girl to such a fate, much less the charming little Sigyn, but Fingardin was right. The sacrifice of this one girl could ensure peace throughout the nine realms for as long as one of her descendants sat upon the throne of Scandia. Besides, how much longer could this creature go on living, anyway? It would be some years before Sigyn came of age; even if

Fingardin lived, he could easily forget such a promise.

"Yes, this is true, but only with a parent's blessing here in Asgard," said Odin. "I believe that any father would be proud to have his daughter marry into such a noble family. Consider it done. You and Sigyn are now betrothed, to be wed upon her reaching womanhood. We all await the happy occasion with great anticipation. And now I see your chariot awaits." Odin urged his guests towards the Bifrost.

"Soon, then, I shall consult the augers, who will inform me of that most special day. Until such time, Odin." Fingardin and his men were quickly swept away through the Bifrost.

Odin stepped wearily away from the Gatekeeper and walked slowly back to the castles of Asgard. He knew that both Frigga and his cousin Arngeirr would be horrified of the deal he had just sworn, but in his heart of hearts, he knew he could have made no other.

The years passed all too quickly. Thor grew ever stronger and had mastered the hammer Mjolnir. Loki had learned the art of conjuring objects out of thin air and had gotten the reputation for being a tremendous prankster. Most of his jokes were harmless, but he could occasionally be downright cruel. A few had actually caused injury. There were many of Odin's court who mistrusted, disliked, and even hated him. But with Sigyn, he was different. He played his jokes on her as well, but they were always harmless and often surprisingly sweet. Their relationship was rapidly changing from a brother and sisterly sort of love to a much more romantic kind. They would both soon be of age, and they fantasized about what it would be like to be married.

"We would do everything together. Horseback riding, hunting, everything," mused

Loki one day, as they lay side by side, staring at clouds in the lazy summer afternoon.

"Washing dishes, doing laundry...everything?" teased Sigyn.

Loki sat up on his elbows. "Nothing so mundane as that – we'd have servants for that. But everything else – share and share alike."

"But we do that already, silly. Why get married, then?" She turned on her side, smiling up at him.

Loki gazed into her deep blue eyes, summoned his courage, and kissed her. He quickly broke apart from her, studying her for a reaction.

Sigyn's smile had turned to a look of surprise. Her mouth turning up into a smile again, she raised her face to his, and they kissed again, this time with real conviction. They soon found themselves rolling about in the warm grass, kissing so deeply they both thought they might fall into one another and become as one forever. Loki began to explore her body with eager hands, and she, too, began to feel her way down his chest, over his abdomen...then suddenly, she stopped. He thought his heart would pound out of his chest, and to his great chagrin, he felt himself let go. He felt the rhythmic spurting from his loins, and the warm wetness spread across his belly.

"Oh, god…" he said. "Oh, god, oh god, oh god…"

"What?" cried Sigyn. "What's wrong?"

"I-it's n-nothing," he stammered, turning away from her. "I j-just, I mean, I...I...I've got to go," he shouted, and ran towards the castle.

One should never tell one's self that things couldn't be worse, because without fail, they immediately are. Just ahead of him, between himself and the castle, sat his brother and his band of friends who were also enjoying the lazy sunshine. He thought of just throwing himself off the nearest cliff, and closing his eyes, wished himself invisible. And then it happened. A queer feeling came over him, like a thousand butterflies lightly flickering their wings against his skin. The next thing he knew, Thor had stood up abruptly, calling out, "Did you see that? Loki? Where'd you go?"

Loki looked down at his hands; they were still there, but, apparently, he was the only one seeing them. He closed his eyes again and pictured himself safely in his room. When he opened them, there he was, standing just inside his bedroom door. He rushed to his mirror and saw....nothing! He was invisible! With some degree of trepidation, he closed his eyes again, wishing himself visible again. Slowly, with a squint, he cracked one eyelid up a fraction of an inch. He was back! Then he remembered his predicament and climbed out of his sodden britches. What a rotten lover *he* was going to make! He would have to run away – he could never see Sigyn again. How could he face her? Her very touch made him explode! He cleaned himself and dragged on fresh clothes. Heartbroken, he threw himself across his bed. A hand laid itself gently across his back.

"Loki," a tentative voice whispered. "Did I just see what I think I saw?" Thor sat down quietly next to his brother.

"I dunno," Loki answered, voice muffled by the covers of his bed.

"You just disappeared," he said, voice in awe. Shouting, he boomed, "You just effing disappeared!" With a whoop, he jumped up on his brother's bed, and began wildly hopping up and down. "You're amazing! No, astounding! No, you're effing *fantastic*!" he shouted.

"Yeah, sure, I'm an effing *god*," replied Loki quietly from his sheets.

Thor plopped himself down next to his brother. "Look," he began, "I don't think anybody else noticed that you'd wet your pants, and besides, who cares? You. Can. Effing. *Disappear!*"

Loki turned himself enough to see his brother's grinning face. "You noticed that, did you? That's effing great," he sighed, and buried his face deeper into the mattress again.

The next day was Monday, and time to go back to classes again. If Loki had any thoughts that his brother had kept his secret to himself at all, he was about to be sorely disappointed. Thor's friend Sif stopped him before he entered the classroom, asking him if perhaps he might want to make a stop at the bathroom first. Then, instead of his usual seat, someone had replaced it with a portable wooden

John, hole in the seat and all. He heard the snickering from Thor's other buddies, Fandral, Hogun, and Valstagg, echoing down the hallway.

Sigyn had her head down, furiously studying something in her textbook.

Thor was staring innocently into space. "Good morning, brother," he offered, cheerily.

Loki suddenly brightened a little, answering, "Good morning it is, dear brother," before pulling his regular chair back into place. Thor flipped open his textbook as it lay on his desk, only to have no less than six large crows fly out from the pages into his face. "Yes, good morning indeed," Loki smiled as he sat himself down.

Arms still flapping to insure that he wouldn't be attacked by more birds, Thor glared at his brother. "Not funny," he spat.

"Dunno," replied Loki. "Funny as an empty toilet, anyway."

Sigyn had looked up from her book and was smiling at Loki. "Good one," she whispered to him.

At that moment, Loki was sure he was in love.

Syr rapped her knuckles on the top of her big oak desk. "Alright, class, today we're going to attempt to change lead into gold." She looked over the tops of her half-moon glasses for her students' reactions. They were quite used to her strange pronouncements by now, so no surprise registered on their faces.

Thor's hand flew up. "Loki learned how to disappear, Ma'am," he offered.

Somewhat taken aback, Syr stared at Loki quizzically before asking, "Is this true, Loki?"

Cheeks reddening, "Yes," Loki replied.

The teacher slowly rose, not taking her eyes off her young student. "Come with me," she stated. "The rest of you, read pages 347 through 411 of 'The Alchemist's Guide to Wealth and Fortune.'"

Apprehensively, Loki stood and left the classroom with his teacher. He was afraid that he was in some sort of trouble and began to think about turning invisible again.

Syr stopped and bent over and stared at him, eye to eye. "I see great potential in you, Loki. You have the makings of a great sorcerer."

Loki wasn't sure what to say. He knew a few tricks, and except for the invisibility, and now the teleportation, they seemed like useless powers at best. "I'm not so sure of that," he replied sheepishly.

Syr stared hard into his face. "Great sorcerer," she repeated. "Have you tried anything else?"

He looked at his feet. "Well, I did sort of pop off from the lawn into my bedroom...but it was while I was invisible, so I don't think I can do it again."

The teacher snatched him to her breast, almost smothering him with her hugs. "Oh, Loki, Loki, Loki!! You wonderful, wonderful boy!! Actually, there's little I can teach you. Most of your magic will come from your mind and your heart. These are the basics....all life is made of energy. And particles. All life is made of energy and particles. Some few, that is to say, *very* few, are able to tap into that energy and, thus, manipulate the particles. You just need to want it, to feel it, and to will it to happen."

Loki was a little embarrassed. He had always felt different, but he wasn't sure he wanted these "wonderful" powers. He listened anyway and tried to understand what Syr was saying.

"Look at your hand. It is made of millions of tiny particles. And what surrounds you hand? Not empty space – *more* particles!" She began to wave her hand slowly forwards and back. "Feel that?" she asked. "That softness, that cool breeziness as you wave your hand – you are compressing and releasing millions of atoms, all of which contain energy, so much energy that if you were to split just one of them this entire castle would be destroyed."

She lay her hand against the wall. "Why doesn't my hand sink through this wall?" Loki stared, unable to think of an answer. "It's because all of these particles carry a charge. Like charges repel, opposite charges attract. The particles of this wall are quite dense, and they are repelling the particles of your hand. But if you will those particles to change their charge..." Her hand began to sink into the wall. "...then there is nothing repelling your hand anymore." She drew her hand back out from the wall. "Once you've practiced a bit, it will be so natural, you'll hardly have to think about it all."

Loki stared at her, dumbfounded. "Why me?" he asked. "Why can't everybody do this? 'Just will the particles to change'...you know that's absurd." He smacked his hand against the wall, its particles stinging the palm of his hand, thank you very much.

Syr smiled at him. "You have to want it, Loki. Do you want your hand to pass through the wall?" she asked.

Loki thought about it. 'Not really,' he thought to himself. Then, he looked at Syr's kind face, knowing all she wanted was to see him succeed at something. She had seen Thor win so many competitions, seen Odin beam with pride at his exceptional son, while Loki had struggled with all his might just to keep up. So he wanted it. He thought of the particles. He thought of the hardness of the wall, then he began to think about the air he had passed his hand through so effortlessly. Then he imagined the wall was just like the air, and—"I did it," he whispered, as his hand floated through the stone as though dipping into water.

* * *

The next few weeks were magical indeed for young Loki. Now that he knew what he was doing, his conjuring tricks had become much more elaborate. He was able to create what looked like live snakes or spiders at will, having them crawl across people's shoes or drop down onto people's heads. He could make doors appear or disappear in the middle of corridors, cause a step to vanish beneath one's foot, or have one's britches fall suddenly to the floor. He walked through walls and doors as if walking through air. And, finally, he discovered what he felt to be his most amazing feat of all. He could shift himself into other people or animals and back again. He was deep in adolescence and very sexually curious. He and Sigyn had resumed their passionate kissing and fondling, and he had found new self-control when aroused by her. But that was as far as they had gotten. When he had pressed her to go further, she had rebuffed him soundly. She wasn't giving up her virginity until her wedding night, and that was that!

"My god, I love you so much," he had said to her, as they lay together under the moonlight.

"I love you, too, Loki. You and no other, ever, forever," she had replied. As he gazed onto her eyes, he knew that she meant it, with all her heart and soul.

It was then that he had gotten really curious. He wondered if his caresses were as pleasurable for her as they were for him. His brother, Thor, had bragged about his many conquests, and how his women had swooned at his very touch. He had always been jealous of Thor, and now he felt he had to know his brother's special techniques. Sigyn had *never* swooned. She had shivered and sighed, and he thought she may have stopped breathing for a while once, but she had certainly never "swooned."

That was when he wanted it. He wanted to know what Thor's women felt. He had to know, first hand, what it was like. As he wanted it, he felt himself begin to change. He felt his chest begin to swell, and his groin began to ache. His bones felt lighter, and his throat began to constrict. Suddenly, the strange pains and sensations stopped. The most obvious change was right in front of him – he had grown breasts! Very ample breasts, at that. Tentatively, he slowly slipped his hand down towards his crotch, and... He yanked his hand back and began to sweat. What if he couldn't change back? Could he live out the rest of his life as a...a...a girl?? He was sure Sig wouldn't like it, or at least he was pretty sure; maybe she was curious, too...

He stood up, and crept towards his mirror. The face that stared back at him was not his; yet, somehow it was. His throat was slender, and his jaw not so pronounced. His hair was longer and thicker. His waist more narrow, his lips and hips, fuller. All in all, he was not unattractive, he told himself. But his clothes were all wrong. He had to find something to wear...

Ever so quietly, he tiptoed into his mother's bedchamber. A silky robe lay across a chair. He picked it up and crept silently back into his own room. There, he stripped off his clothes and slid into the slinky robe. He heard Thor's confident stride clomping up the hallway towards his own bedroom, closing the door behind him. Loki fluffed his hair a little and cautiously approached his brother's chambers. He rapped ever so gently at his door.

"Yes, who is it?" Thor asked.

At first, Loki was tempted to try to raise his voice to some more feminine level, but at the last moment chose to speak in his own voice. "It's me," he whispered, happy to hear some teenage girl's voice twitter out of him. "I have to see you...to, well, *be* with you," he continued.

Thor cracked open the door. He didn't recognize this new girl, but he was used to them falling all over themselves to try to get his attention. This one was adorable, to boot. "Come on in," he invited.

For Loki, it was all he could do not to burst into laughter. But his brother's hands were on his breasts now, and it just felt so damn good!! "Oh, Thor," he moaned. "Don't stop."

Thor obliged, and began kissing his brother, deeply. Loki admitted to himself that Thor's kisses weren't all that great, but he did have a way with his hands.

Thor slipped the robe off Loki's shoulders, leaving him stark naked. He grabbed him by the buttocks and lifted him to his waist. Loki wrapped his legs around him, and the two of them headed towards the bed. Thor tossed him onto the bed and climbed on top of him. Loki couldn't help himself...he was giggling, now laughing out loud. Thor laughed with him, thinking this was one of the most delightful girls he had had in quite a while. Thor was fondling him, but Loki pushed his hand away. He didn't want to lose his virginity to his big brother.

"Oh, no you don't," he giggled. Loki was having second thoughts. He thought about shifting back, but then his brother began to stroke him between his thighs, and he decided he might wait just a little bit longer. Then, Thor became more aggressive; Loki thought his brother might actually rape him. All of a sudden, Thor grabbed him, and flipped him onto his belly.

"Wha – what are you doing?" Loki asked with some apprehension.

"Just relax," reassured Thor. "You're going to love it."

Loki was pretty sure he was not, and reached behind him to push his brother away. "I said NO!" His voice boomed, which finally got Thor's attention. Suddenly, there was a burst of light in the room, and Loki realized that the door must have swung open. He was aware that his breasts had shrink back into his chest. He propped himself up on his elbows and turned his head to look at the door. And there, in the doorway, was his father, with the strangest look Loki had ever seen on his face.

"Oh, hello father," Loki said in his usual masculine voice.

Thor looked down on in horror on Loki's back, realizing what he was about to do. He made a sort of strangling noise and ran to vomit in the nearest basin.

Loki turned full to face his father now, and grinned at him. "This was all just a little experiment, Father....you see, a moment ago, I was a woman. Syr has taught me to manipulate my particles, and..."

Odin's face was so red, Loki thought it might burst into flame. "You what?" he roared.

"Syr taught you what?" he roared again.

Thor looked daggers in Loki's direction. He heaved again in the direction of the basin before turning to face his brother. "You've done some awful things, brother, but whatever possessed you to pull a thing like this?"

"Pull what? Your penis?" Loki laughed.

Thor puked again before turning on his brother. "Get out of my room, Loki, before I wring your pathetic little neck," Thor pronounced.

Loki smiled as he rose from the bed. "What? No goodnight kiss?" he asked, and immediately transported himself back into his own bedroom, wisely locking the door behind him.

* * *

Except for the exile of Syr, nothing seemed to change around Asgard after "the joke," as Loki preferred to call it. He knew why, of course. No one wanted the Asgardians to know that their future King just about had some hot, nasty sex with his own brother. Loki also suspected that Thor might have secretly enjoyed it a little; Loki was pretty sure Thor would screw just about anything, and he thought his brother had looked at him just a bit too long in the shower on occasion or two. Whatever the reason, things began to return to normal again.

Loki missed his old teacher, but Thor assured him Odin hadn't sent her somewhere too horrible. Thanks to his brother Thor, Loki felt more assured that he wouldn't be such a bad lover and vowed always to be considerate of Sigyn's needs and never to force himself on her. What Loki wanted more than anything was to please her, not the other way round.

Loki's birthday had come and gone, and in two days, Sigyn would celebrate hers. The Great Hall was decorated, people invited, menus planned. Loki had been teaching himself in secret to fly, so that his gift to her would be to fly her anywhere her heart desired. Everyone took it for granted that, when they were of age, Loki and Sigyn would be married. As they sat together at dinner, Frigga would pat Odin's hand and say, "They make a lovely couple, don't they?" Odin would smile back at her, ever glad to be assured that Loki did like girls, after all.

Loki visited Sig in her room. He found her lying on her stomach, apparently in some pain. She glanced up at him, and turned away.

"Go away," she commanded.

Loki was taken aback. Sig had never demanded he leave her, especially for absolutely no reason that he could imagine. "Whatever it is, I didn't do it," he insisted.

"This isn't about you, Loki. Why does everything have to be about you? I just need to be alone, that's all." Tears welled in her eyes.

Loki hesitated, then turned to go.

Sig turned quickly to face him. "You're leaving?" she implored. She looked as though she was in great anguish. "I can't believe you're just going to leave me like this!" she shouted

Loki's jaw dropped. "But – but – you just....you told me to go..." he stammered.

"But you're supposed to know I didn't mean it!" she wailed.

"Sig, what's going on? What can I do?" a look of concern covered Loki's face.

Sig sat up, and took Loki's hand. "It came today," she sniffled.

Now Loki was frightened. What could have arrived that was causing his beautiful Sigyn so much pain? He sat next to her and embraced her. "Whatever it is, I'll protect you.

I'll see that you're rid of it, and it never comes again," he assured her.

Loki thought he felt more sobs shaking Sig's thin frame, when he heard her low chuckle begin to grow.

"Would that you could do such a thing," she laughed. "No, my dearest, today, I have become a woman. And it's awful. Frigga says she has potions that will help. I'm sorry I was so curt with you. It seems one moment I'm fine, and the next, I want to rip out the throat of the next person who dares to speak to me." She laid her head on his chest and sighed.

Loki wasn't sure what he was supposed to do, so he simply hugged her. He also decided that transforming into a woman might not be so much fun, after all.

*   *   *

A week later, a message arrived from Fingardin. "Congratulations, my sweet. Today you are a woman. Tomorrow is your wedding day. Your betrothed, Lord Fingardin."

The house of Asgard was in complete turmoil. Odin had been sure that the old man would be dead by now, or at least so senile as to forget he ever had a bride coming to him. Arngeirr refused to give consent. Odin begged, pleaded, cajoled, all to no avail. Finally, he threatened. Arngeirr was to give his consent willingly, or, as King, Odin would assume his right to claim her and give his consent himself. Arngeirr said that was what would have to be, because he would *never* give his beloved Sigyn over to that brute, Fingardin.

Loki fumed. He would never, *ever* allow anyone to take his Sig from him. He stalked his room, beat his floor until his fists bled, begged his father, and screamed at the heavens, but nothing could relieve the pain in his heart. Sigyn was resigned to her fate. Odin had come to her, tears running down his face. "It is the only way, my dear, that we can maintain peace between our nation and that of Jotunheim. May God forgive me, but it is the only way."

She had taken his hands in hers and gently kissed him on his cheek. "It will be alright, My Lord. Like you said before, he can't live much longer. And then, Loki and I will finally be together." The girl was breaking his heart. Odin left her, the burden of knowing what he had done to her weighing on him so heavily he thought he might collapse and sink through the floor.

Sigyn sat on her bed next to Loki. Both had faces swollen and streaked with tears. "I have a plan," began Sigyn. "You know of my songs. I will sing Fingardin to sleep each night and fill his head with such vivid dreams that he will feel sure he has had me. In reality, he will never even touch me." She clutched her lover's arm, more to reassure him than herself

"They'll want proof," Loki said. "They'll look for blood. They'll look for proof that he took you...took your....," he whispered.

Sigyn picked up a dagger from beside her bed. "Then I'll hide this beneath my gown, and when I'm sure he's asleep, I'll pierce myself, and smear the blood on him, and all will be convinced."

Loki turned pained eyes on her, then stared at the floor, thinking. "Perhaps there's a better way. Once he's asleep, you can sneak down into the kitchen. There should be birds somewhere nearby, birds for cooking, but still living. You can take one of the birds to your room, then pierce its heart and pour its blood over him and his bed. That way you can save yourself…" He paused. "…for me." He looked anxiously at her, and she threw her arms around him.

"Tomorrow, Loki, as I am forced to recite those vows, when I speak his name with my lips, I shall say your name in my mind, and I will be your wife, not his!"

"And when they ask him to speak his vows, I shall speak them with my heart, and you will ever be my wife, not his!" They clutched at each other as if never to let go. They were still barely children, but they felt as if their lives were over. They couldn't imagine anything more tragic could ever happen to either of them. They fell asleep that way, holding on to each other as if for dear life itself.

The dawn came all too quickly. Frigga found the two still clinging to one another and, with tear-filled eyes, forced them apart. "I'm sorry, Sigyn, but it is time for you to get ready."

Tears welling, with broken voice, Loki begged, "Mother, no," but she wrenched his arms away from his lover and pushed him from the room.

Loki fell to the floor outside her door, sobbing, broken, empty.

Thor crouched beside him. "I am so very sorry, my brother," he whispered. "I know how much you love one another. But think, Loki. You are not without powers. There must be something you can do. I'll gather my friends, and we'll go to Scandia and slaughter them all!" he shouted.

Loki's sad eyes fell on his brother's angry, determined face. "I believe you would," he said. "But if we kill the Fingardins, then there will surely be war. Thousands will die. Innocents, used as shields by the Fingardins and

Laufey. You speak what I scream from my heart, but we cannot. We cannot." Loki's face grew less dark. "But you are right. I do have powers. Perhaps there is a way to have it all, dear brother. Perhaps there is a way yet."

The day of the wedding had arrived. Loki stared hard at the man who would take his Sig as a bride. Fingardin was drunk already, swaying as he waited at the altar. Farting, burping, stinking mass of rotting disgusting flesh. To call him a pig would be to do an injustice to swine.

And then, there she was. Loki wondered to himself, "When had Sig become so beautiful?" Her gown trailed softly behind her. Her lovely flame-red hair was done up softly around her head, decorated with flowers and pearls. Odin walked with her; they both seemed to be holding the other up. Words were said, and when Fingardin was asked if he would take this woman to be his wife, forsaking all others,

Loki whispered, "I do," and when Sigyn was asked if she would take Fingardin to be her husband, forsaking all others, she looked straight into Loki's eyes, and replied, "I do," and then mouthed "take thee Loki," for his eyes only.

And then it was over. Fingardin rushed his new bride out of the hall with far more speed than Loki thought the drunken old man had in him. It was up to Sig, now, Sig, and her beautiful voice. Loki's eyes were hard, as he planned his next move.

The House of Fingardin

Fingardin had not touched her yet. Sigyn tried to appear happy as she was paraded through the front door and into the main hall. Here, there were goats and pigs rutting about. Birds flew about the rafters, their droppings landing on food, drink, and people's heads. The smell was almost unbearable. In one corner lay a dead dog. In another, what appeared to be a dead man. Everyone was drunk, and everyone was shouting.

Fingardin took his seat at the head of the table. He grabbed Sig by the arm and forced her into his lap. His belly was so large, there wasn't much lap on which she could sit. A young serving girl, younger than Sig, brought a tray bearing flagons of ale. A drunken man sitting next to Sigyn grabbed the front of the girl's blouse and ripped it down exposing her breasts. He then grabbed them roughly, commenting to his friends how firm and full they were. The girl was obviously terrified, but no one helped her. The man then positioned himself behind her, hoisted up her skirts, and began to have her right there, on the table. Sigyn tried to look away, but such debauchery was everywhere. The man finished with the girl, and then offered her up to his buddies.

Fingardin must have been aroused by the plight of the serving girl, because he stood up and tried to force his new bride across the table so that he might have her right there as well. The men laughed and cheered their leader on, telling him to "rip the bitch wide open." Sig tried desperately to calm herself, to remove the strain from her voice. Softly, she began to sing. It was a song to Fingardin, a song about a soft lovely bed, and how wonderful it would be to have his wife all to himself up in his very own bed. He lessened the grip he had on Sig's wrists and swayed slightly, as he listened to her sing. Then, with a jolt, he slapped her to the ground.

"Stop that singing, you stupid little bitch. You're confusing me!" he shouted.

She tasted blood, and her mouth stung, but Sigyn continued to sing. Fingardin's eyes drooped slightly, and he began to recite back some of the words of the song. "To bed, to bed my love, and now it's off to bed," he sang. He picked Sigyn up, and threw her across his shoulder. To the crowd, she began to sing of "sleep, restful sleep, all must now go to sleep, sleep, sleep." The drunkards dropped their women, stopped their fighting, and began dropping off to sleep where they sat and where they stood.

To the young serving girl, Sigyn sang that she should go home and sleep now, and all would be healed and forgotten by the morrow. The girl, glassy eyed, wandered out the door, hopefully to a safe place to sleep, to heal, and to forget.

Fingardin kicked open a door at the top of the steps. In one corner of the room was a large and filthy bed. He tossed her on the bed the way one might toss a sack of potatoes onto a kitchen table. She continued to sing, inviting him to lay down beside her and sleep, sleep, sleep. In just a few moments, he was snoring quietly, his face to the wall. Sig brought her knees up to her face and hugged them with her arms, her head bowed, and she sobbed. She was of royal blood. She had always had nice things around her; fresh linens, clean sheets and clothes, genteel people. She was sure that she was in Hell.

Steadying herself, she removed the dagger she had kept hidden under her clothing. She thought about the poor bird she must sacrifice just to prove to some nosy lawyer that she had allowed this pig to deflower her, and then she thought about piercing her own heart, instead. "Oh, Loki," she whispered.

"Yes, my love?" came a voice from the shadows. Slowly, Loki sauntered from the darkest corner of the room and stood by her bedside. Sig dropped her dagger and threw her arms around him. He engulfed her in his own and lifted her off the floor. "Why murder some poor bird, when we can find another source of blood to satisfy the council of the King?" He smiled wryly down at her. "After all, you did say you were saving yourself for me, did you not?"

They tore at each other's clothes, until they were standing naked in front of one another. Loki's eyes flashed as he touched the bruises on her arms and face. She touched her fingers to her lips, and then to his. "From this point on, only words of love will be spoken here, for this is my wedding bed, and I shall have it no other way."

Loki smiled at her, kissing her gently on the lips. Their kisses became more urgent, hungrier. He lowered her to the bed, caressing her; she wrapped her legs around him, and then he was inside her. At last, they were together, completely. They were not the least shy with one another, and tried daring, tortuous positions and often fell apart laughing at one another, only to unite again, and again, and again. The room began to lose its darkness, and Sigyn grabbed Loki so tightly, he thought she might have actually bruised a rib. But he did not protest, and he held her right back, knowing only too well what was to come next.

"I have to go," he said softly.

"I know, "she replied, her face buried in his chest. "Leave something with me, something that smells of you, so that I might close my eyes and crush it to my face and, if only for a moment, I might feel I'm with you again."

Loki ripped a sleeve from his shirt and handed it to her. "Your scent is everywhere at home. It's on your pillow, the sheets of your bed, the clothes you left behind. You're everywhere around me, but you're not there. I think that I'll go mad without you."

They clutched at each other again, the light growing ever brighter. "I'll sing a song of hunting to him today. I'll convince him to stay away for weeks, maybe months. We will be together, Loki. Nothing will ever keep us totally apart."

"I'll be back tonight. You can tell me if your new plan succeeded. I love you, Sig. There will never be another."

"And I love you, Loki, no other, ever and forever."

With that, Loki stepped back into the darkened corner of the room and was gone.

*   *   *

The next few weeks were glorious for Sigyn and Loki. Sig's songs had convinced Fingardin that he needed to take a large party of hunters far into the north to hunt for Polar Bears. Sig sang to the drunkards camped out in the Fingardin lodge, telling them of their overwhelming need to earn an honest living and support their wives and families. With the help of Loki's magic, she had the enormous log structure cleaned and polished. All the animals were relegated to the outdoors and to the barns that dotted the countryside.

Loki and Sigyn were even so bold as to take walks into the village, where they learned of the great strife caused by Fingardin's dictatorial rule. Families were frequently torn apart to supply the slaves the Elves demanded in exchange for weaponry. Sigyn sang to them about freedom and vowed to end the slave trade forever. She provided food and shelter to the needy and medicine and simple healing potions to the sick. The people loved her, and with the constant encouragement from their new queen and her "bodyguard," they began to have hope again. They repaired their homes and better tended their crops and livestock.

Sadly, it was time again for the return of Fingardin and his hunting party. The parting between Loki and Sigyn was not quite so bitter this time; they both knew that they would see one another again. Sigyn had already composed a song about pirate treasure to send her husband off to somewhere far in the southern seas. She sang him to sleep again that night, and, again, her beloved Loki appeared to her, and they slept in each other's arms yet another blissful evening.

*   *   *

It wasn't long before Sigyn noticed some changes within her. She was woozy and sometimes nauseated when she first woke up. She felt more tired and irritable than at any time she could remember. Then, it occurred to her she must be pregnant.

Fingardin had just returned to the sea, so she had the time and the privacy to deliver the news to Loki. She was afraid he would be angry with her, but his reaction was one of the greatest pride and joy.

"A baby, Sig. A baby! Our baby! I only hope he takes after you. The gods forbid another child might be born with a face like this," he pointed to his own visage.

Sigyn placed her hands on either side of her lover's face. "Loki, my Loki. When I gaze upon you, I gaze upon heaven itself." She smiled and kissed him lightly on both cheeks.

Loki ran his hands through her beautiful flame red hair. "Fingardin's hair is red, too. Your father and his both had black hair like mine, didn't they?" His expression showed some slight apprehension.

Sigyn understood his meaning. "Yes, when our son is born with his father's raven hair, I will simply convince Fingardin that the coloring skips a generation. He has no reason to doubt. He thinks he has me for hours each night as he sleeps here with me." She smiled and took his hand. "It will be alright, My Lord," she said. "Once the old man is finally dead, we will reveal the truth about our son. Things have changed; the weapons have been returned in secret to the Elves, and those poor souls they enslaved, those still living, have returned to their homes. Fingardin has been too wrapped up in search for treasure to even notice."

"Then why don't you leave him now? Go to Odin and beg for an annulment from this loveless marriage. Then, we can finally be married for real," Loki said.

Sigyn's smile was sad as she took her lover's hand. "Not yet, Loki. As long as Fingardin lives, there is the awful chance that a spell might be broken, and he would return to rule here in his horrid, cruel way. Be patient, my love. It will happen." She reached up and caressed the side of his face.

Loki took her hand and kissed her palm, holding it there, not wishing the moment to ever end. "I try to be patient, Sig; I have tried to be patient my whole life." He sighed when he saw the look of pain in Sigyn's eyes. "But," he began, "I will be patient just a little while longer. For you," he added.

* * *

Fingardin returned, and he had in fact found a small casket of gold bullion and jewels. With this success, it took very little convincing on Sigyn's part to get him back out to sea again. Unfortunately, life at sea seemed to agree with Fingardin. He grew healthier and stronger with each trip. On the other hand, his travels took him away for months, allowing her to continue her benevolent rule of Scandia and live blissfully with Loki. Fingardin had been sorely unimpressed with the news that his bride was with child, and so he made no effort to return in time for its birth.

Loki insisted that Sigyn return to Asgard for the birth of their child. He knew full well that he had to continue the deceit, to continue to pretend that this baby was not his own, but Fingardin's. Thor was thrilled to have his brother around for a while. Loki had been away so much these days. He said it was to improve his skills as a Master Sorcerer, but Thor was still sad to see him gone for weeks and even months at a time.

Sigyn was attended by Frigga and her maids. The Queen commented on Sigyn's girth, and predicted twins. Sigyn turned quite white at the thought, but tried to keep herself calm. Labor began the third night she was back at Asgard. Loki begged for the right to be with her to comfort her, and seeing that this was the young girl's first child, Frigga was inclined to indulge him. As the pains became stronger,

Loki was beside himself, being unable to relieve his beloved Sig of her pain. When at last a head began to emerge, and Sigyn let out an almost guttural scream as she pushed, Loki screamed with her. To his shock, the child first appeared blue. The midwife assured the mother that this often happened with first babies, and she rubbed the tiny boy until his skin grew increasingly pink.

"You were right, my Queen," stated the midwife. "Here's the second one coming now! Push, milady, *push!*" she demanded.

Sigyn protested that she was too tired, that she couldn't do it, that she just wanted to rest. The midwife insisted again that she push hard, or the baby could die. Loki gripped her hand and whispered into her ear. "You can do this, my love. You are the strongest woman I know. Now, please, my Sig, my love, *push!*"

Sigyn took several breaths, and staring into Loki's eyes, she gathered all her strength and *pushed*! A second boy, also tinged blue, burst into the room and let out a wail. The nurse rubbed the child like she had the first, and he, too, became pink. Both boys had headfuls of inky, black hair. Loki stared, fascinated by the two wriggling, wailing babies. "Two sons," he thought. "I have two sons," and he wanted to shout it out to the world, but he could not. He asked to hold the first child, his firstborn son, and carried him tenderly to his mother.

"He's quite beautiful," he whispered, tears trickling down his face. "They both are," he assured his beloved Sigyn.

She cradled them, one on each arm. She signaled for Loki to lean close. "Of course they are," she whispered. "They both look just like their father." He kissed her softly, and then pulled away just as the midwife returned to Sig's side. "Come, come now, the lady needs her rest. We can take care of her now," she said, gently pushing Loki out the door.

Loki begged Sigyn to stay at Asgard until her husband returned from sea, but she expressed the desire to return as soon as possible. In one of the few moments they were alone together, Sigyn said, "The more we are all seen together, the sooner people will look at the boys and put two and two together. I've arranged for my own nurse at Fingardin's, and there, you can be their father, openly. The people there would only love us more if they knew that hated old tyrant hadn't produced any heirs. Make your excuses, and come as soon as you can. We shall all miss you." They stole a quick kiss just before the nurse returned with the squalling children.

"Sorry, milady, but it's feeding time again." Sigyn sat down in one of the overstuffed chairs of the bed chamber as the nurse helped place a child at each breast. "Growing fast, they are. They'll be tall ones, like your friend there…" The nurse stopped mid-sentence, her cheeks turning pink. "I didn't mean to say, milady... I mean..."

Sigyn spoke softly to the old nurse, her words coming out almost song like, "My father, and his father before him, they both had raven black hair, and they were as tall as trees. It is my father they most resemble, it seems."

The nurse smiled and nodded slowly. "Of course, their grandfather... They look just like him, they do." With that, she sat in a chair nearby, in case milady needed anything from her.

*   *   *

Fingardin returned but was ill. He slept in his own sick room away from Sigyn and the children, so Sigyn didn't have to place any spell upon him, this time. His brutish friends stayed there in the lodge, however, so Loki was forced to stay away. He did come stealthily one night, but his presence woke the babies, and their plaintive cries woke one of the cretins sleeping nearby. He banged on the door shouting, "Shut those damned whelps up or I'll shut 'em up for ya," and then headed down the hall. Loki turned the hallway floor to ice, and the oaf slid all the way down to the steps, which he could have sworn the next day that he had been kicked down.

The old man stayed for months, and the months turned to years. Sigyn managed to sing the brutish guests away, so Loki was able to visit more often. Sometimes, Sigyn would take the children for walks down to the village, where "Uncle Loki" would meet up with them, grab them up, and swing them around till they felt as though they were flying. One day, Sig found Vali spinning himself around like a top. Suddenly, his feet left the ground, and he hovered in midair for several seconds. "See, Mother," he cried. "Just like Uncle Loki!" Then, he lightly touched ground. This sort of behavior would be irrefutable proof at last that Loki was indeed their father.

Loki and Sigyn had argued about revealing the truth to his sons. Loki feared for the lives of the two boys and of Sigyn. But now, Sigyn felt she had to talk with them, to let them know how important it was to keep their magic, and their birthright, a secret. Loki wasn't supposed be there again until tomorrow, so Sigyn decided to follow her instincts and have a talk with her sons. She called them into her chambers, and sat them down.

Vali was the eldest (by about three minutes) and by far the boldest. His younger brother, Narfi, was much quieter and more thoughtful. "Are you angry with me, mother? Don't you like it that I can fly?" Vali asked.

Narfi looked down at his hands resting quietly in his lap. "It's supposed to be a secret, Vali. No one but mother and Loki should ever see us doing magic." He raised his eyes up to look into his mother's. "Isn't that right, Mummy?" he asked.

The two were as identical as if one had stepped out of a mirror gazed into by the other, but they appeared as unique and individual to Sigyn as two boys born years apart. Narfi had the sad, haunted eyes of his father. Vali had his father's eyes, as well, but they seemed to constantly sparkle as Loki's did when he was about to play some joke on someone. Sigyn stroked each boy's hair, and felt her heart swell as she gazed at them. A memory stirred within her, a memory of her very first friend when she had come to learn at Asgard, a memory of a young schoolboy, Loki. She wondered if there was any of her blood in either of them.

"You're right, Narfi, but do you know why?" The boys looked at each other, but offered no answer. She tried to prepare her words carefully. "Do you love Loki?" she asked. Both boys nodded enthusiastically. "And you know that he loves you, too, don't you?" Again, the vigorous nods.

"Of course he loves us, Mummy; he's our Dad," said Narfi.

Sigyn was speechless. "Who told you that?" she demanded.

Vali, who wore his heart on his sleeve, looked hurt. "He is, isn't he, mother? I mean, we're so much alike, and there's a feeling here, in my chest, when I see him. I just know he's our Dad."

Narfi spoke next. "We knew there must be a good reason you wanted us to call him Uncle. We know that he isn't your husband, which makes us bastards, I suppose. You probably don't want anyone to think badly of us, so you've made up this story. This story that we're Fingardin's sons, and Loki, our Dad, is just a friend." The two sat as calmly as though they were discussing their lessons after a day at school.

Sigyn pressed her hands to her face and grinned at her two boys. "You are just like him. You're fully capable of the most complicated deceit. There are those on this planet, you know, who worship Loki as a god, the god of practical jokes and deceit." They grinned at this and poked at each other. "But your father is much more than this. He is wise and caring, and he is one of the most courageous and powerful men I know.

"More powerful than Thor?" asked Vali.

"In his own way, yes, more powerful than Thor," she replied. "But you must promise never to tell anyone, not until some matters here are settled and Odin gives his blessing that your father and I may marry legally. Spiritually, we have always been married. At Fingardin's wedding, when we were asked to take our vows, I spoke Loki's name, and he spoke mine. So you see, you're nobody's bastards," she finished.

"No, we're Loki's sons," proclaimed Vali, proudly.

"You mustn't think we're weak, Mummy. We're very strong, like our father." A crooked smile, Loki's smile, crept across Narfi's face.

"Loki's sons!" repeated Vali.

"Loki's sons!" they shouted in unison.

At that moment, Loki stepped from the shadows in a dark corner of the room. His face was grave. "What's all this?" he demanded.

"It's alright, Father," Narfi said. "We can keep a secret. We've known you were our Dad for years."

"Years." piped in Vali.

"It was obvious. You hair is black, our hair is black, Fingardin's hair is red. You're tall and thin. We're tall and thin. Fingardin's short and fat. You're brilliant, we're brilliant, and Fingardin's an ass." Narfi crossed his arms as he stared up at his father, looking for everything like a miniature Loki.

Loki wanted to be stern. He wanted to scold them all for knowing a dreadful secret that could ruin their lives if leaked out too soon. But the serious face of his son, the youngest brother, like himself, staring him earnestly in the eye was more than he could bear. First he grinned, and then he let out a laugh that rang like music throughout the room.

His laughter was infectious. First, Vali burst out with his high pitched chuckle, then Sigyn laughed, nervously at first, and then all out. Narfi remained grave, until he was unable to hide the twitch at the corners of his mouth. He, too, began to giggle and laugh with the rest of them. It felt to Loki that it had been years since he had laughed like this, especially when it wasn't even at someone else's expense.

Dark Times Again

One morning, as Sigyn was preparing to take the boys to the village for sweets, Fingardin stepped out of his chambers and blocked her way. "And just where are you going, wench?" he asked, his eyes dark and suspicious.

"It's Tuesday, m'lord, and I always take the children into the village for sweet treats on Tuesdays," she replied warily.

"What's been happening here? Where's my gold?" Fingardin demanded.

Thinking Fingardin would never be well enough to leave his bed, Sigyn had used most of the gold to build schools, and a small clinic in the village. As innocently as possible, she asked, "What do you mean, m'lord? The rations you give me are quite ample. I have no need for gold." The boys stepped tall in front of their mother as if to protect her.

"I think I saw that fellow Sigmund walking out of here carrying some sort of box or casket," offered Narfi.

"Oh, yeah," added Vali. "I think he said something about a horse."

Fingardin let out a yell, and demanded his manservant bring him his mount. "That bastard, Sigmund! I never did trust that blackguard. Too tall, too thin." His eyes drifted towards his two sons. "Go on, go get your precious cakes," he shouted, and summarily dismissed them.

"I don't think that worm will ever die," Sigyn proclaimed. "Poor Sigmund. I don't like the idea that some innocent should take the blame for my actions," said Sigyn, thoughtfully.

"Oh, Sigmund's not so innocent, mum. And besides, he's dead. He refused to make good on a bet at the horse races, and a man struck him down," explained Narfi.

"Mother," started Vali, "We've heard some talk. The nurse was crying one day, and she said something about a place called Jotunheim. Narfi thinks they've sent a message to Fingardin, offering him weapons again. The nurse was crying, because her husband was sold to the Elves for weapons, and he died in the mines."

"Mummy won't let that happen," stated Narfi. "Will you, Mummy?" He looked up at her with his soulful eyes.

"The illness seems to have done something to Fingardin's hearing. My song doesn't have much effect on him anymore. He may not be so bold now as to round up people from the village, but he may start abducting them from the countryside. I think we'll need Odin's help with this. Fingardin is mostly powerless now, but if we wait, he could gather his forces again." She pursed her lips in thought.

Narfi piped up, "It's Odin's birthday next week. Maybe you can convince him that Odin wants to give him a gift as part of his celebration. Once he's in Asgard, he can be tried and convicted for his crimes against his people and stripped of his realm."

"How do you know so much about the law?" his mother asked in astonishment.

"I like to read," Narfi replied.

That evening, Sigyn was especially gracious towards her husband, Fingardin. "There's to be such a wonderful party next week. Odin's birthday. I hear there will be wild boar from the very depths of Svartalfheim. There's a rumor that Odin is employing his servant girls from a nunnery. It is also said that he will be honoring his guests with lavish gifts this year." She looked for some sort of response from Fingardin, but all he did was stuff his face with roast lamb and beer. So she began her song, hoping to convince him this one last time

Fingardin stopped chewing abruptly. He straightened his back, and then suddenly let out a huge and windy sneeze. He wiped his mucous covered face on his sleeve, and glanced up at his wife. She continued to sing, and he looked at her as if seeing her for the first time that evening. He began to hum a little back, so she knew at last, the song was reaching him.

"You had better pack tonight," he began. "We're going to Asgard. Odin's birthday. Should be great," he slurred, sloshing down more beer.

The Return to Asgard

The party from the House of Fingardin was much smaller than it had been on the occasion of Fingardin's marriage to Sigyn. There were Fingardin and Sig, their two children, the nurse, a lady's maid, two manservants, and four smallish leather trunks. They were met at the Bifrost by Odin's guards and escorted into the castle. Fingardin was acutely aware of his lack of refinement here and decided to go straight to the food tables, to avoid the invited guests as much as possible. Sigyn, however, displayed the proper etiquette by walking down the center aisle to present herself and her family to the Royal Family of Odin.

Odin, Frigga, Thor, and Loki stood on the center platform, raised high above the crowd. As the little party approached, conversations ceased. Heads turned first to Sigyn and the boys, then to Loki. Loki tried to look as though they were no different than any other guests. Thor began to grin, and poked his brother's side with an elbow. "Lot of schools of sorcery in Scandia, are there?" he smirked.

Noticing the sudden quiet that had overtaken the Hall, Fingardin turned to face the royal podium. The food dropped from his hand as he stared first at Loki, then at the boys, then back at Loki again. At that moment, it all fell into place. He remembered everything. Sigyn had suggested the hunting trips, the treasure hunts. He knew that the sex he thought he had been having with his young wife was much too athletic for him to have actually participated. Loki, the Prankster. They had made a fool of him, laughing at him behind his back, eating his food, stealing his riches.

"Odin!" he bellowed. "I demand justice! My wife is a whore, and these children are the bastard sons of Loki!" He pushed the guests roughly aside, drawing his sword as he marched toward Odin's platform. Thor held Loki, pulling him back.

"Let Odin handle this," he was saying in Loki's ear. But before Loki could break free, Fingardin had reached his bride, and was bearing his sword down on her beautiful neck. The sword was abruptly stayed; two young boys seemed to be hanging from it, but were in fact hovering above the floor, gripping the sword so tightly, their hands bled. Then, the sword began to glow and smoke, and within seconds, it was nothing but ash.

"See that!" Fingardin shouted. "Sons of the Sorcerer! Whore! *Whore!*" he screamed at Sigyn. Sigyn rushed to her sons to see the damage to their hands, only to find that they had healed as quickly as the sword had disintegrated. Loki surrounded them both, wanting to protect them from the gaping eyes of the guests and the rantings of Fingardin.

"I demand satisfaction!" roared Fingardin.

"If it's a duel you want," spat Loki, "then let's be at it!"

Odin smacked his staff hard upon the marble floor, the ensuing crack echoing loudly throughout the Great Hall. "Quiet!" he demanded. The hall was in silence. "Loki, is this true? Have you committed adultery with this woman?" He glared at his youngest son. Adultery was not tolerated within the royal family, and the punishment was banishment, usually to the most unpleasant reaches of all the realms.

Sigyn's voice rang out. "I tricked him, my King. I used my song to entice him. I wanted to punish Thor, who had rebuffed me. I was trapped in a loveless marriage to this hideous man, and I craved the companionship of someone," she paused, "cleaner." She sneered in the direction of Fingardin. "Thor never showed any interest in me, but Loki here, he was like some small puppy, following me everywhere, getting under my feet. I knew it would be easy to cast my spell upon him, and I did. I seduced him into my bed. He was under my control. He could not refuse." She lowered her eyes, refusing to look at Loki.

Odin was quick to seize the opportunity Sigyn had presented him, to both exonerate his son and to distance the royal family from scandal. "The law is clear. Take her to the gatekeeper, and banish her to the farthest corner of the realm. Take her and her illegitimate spawn." With that, he rapped his staff against the marble once more, and his guards ushered Sigyn and the twins away.

Loki couldn't believe what he was seeing. His father was sending his family away forever, perhaps to die in some hostile wilderness. He strained against his brother's mighty grip, and then, suddenly disappeared. Just as quickly, he reappeared in front of Odin, drew his dagger, and made to strike him dead. With a bright blue light and an earsplitting crack, Odin let loose the force of the staff. Loki found himself flat on his back, stunned, unable to raise his arms or legs. "My children. Father. How could you? They are innocents," Loki wailed.

"They share your blood. They are potential heirs to the throne. What's to keep them from seeking revenge some day? It's the law, Loki. In the old days, they would have all been put to death." Odin lowered his staff and approached his son.

"You don't really think she tricked me, do you, Father? Her song has no effect on me. I am the prankster. I am the one who seduced her. She only lied to protect me. We're in love, father. She should have married me!" Loki's body went limp in resignation.

Odin leaned close to Loki's ear, so no one else could hear. "She sacrificed herself and your children to save you, Loki. There are those who want to be rid of you. A charge such as this is all your enemies would need to discredit you, perhaps destroy you. But, Loki, she had to have known that the resemblance between you and the boys could not go unnoticed. Bringing them here was madness."

Loki could hardly find the breath to answer. "I insisted. I was sure we could prove Fingardin's treachery, and that you would demand his immediate execution. I thought... I thought..." His words began to fail him. "I thought that you might then permit us to marry, and I wanted my sons here. I thought..." He could say no more. This was all his fault. Loki the trickster, the master deceiver; how could he not have foreseen this?

Odin left Loki's side and turned to face Fingardin. "Your attempt to take the law into your own hands will not be tolerated in this house. You are hereby ordered to leave at once." He stared down the red faced old man, who decided to back down and go. As it turned out, someone (there are many who credit this to Thor) spread the word to the people of Scandia that their King had been responsible for causing the banishment of their beloved Queen. Before he could return home, Fingardin's house was looted and burned to the ground. As soon as he arrived, Fingardin was captured and put on trial. He was given the choice of death or banishment to parts unknown, never to return again. He chose the latter. In a twist of fate, a few years later, he was aboard a fishing ship that sunk during a great storm. There were no survivors.

Banishment

Sigyn, Vali, and Narfi found themselves in the midst of a snow dusted field. In the distance, they saw some stunted trees, and what looked like smoke curling from someone's chimney. "That looks like our best bet," Sigyn pointed towards what must have been a very tiny cottage at the tree line.

"I'm cold, Mummy," complained Vali.

"Just leave it," snapped Narfi.

"Narfi!" scolded Sigyn. "I'm cold, too, but that house up there has a fire, so the quicker we get there, the sooner we get warm again." She wrapped them in as much of the thin material of her skirts as she could, and the three of them soldiered valiantly on.

The wind was biting and relentless. Sigyn found herself shivering almost uncontrollably. The little house never seemed to grow nearer, and the sun was rapidly setting. She grew steadily more weary and contemplated stopping for just a moment to lay down and rest. She felt her children shivering next to her, so she shut her burning eyes and continued to march.

    A rock caught her foot, and she stumbled to the ground, her boys with her. 'Rest', she thought . 'Just for a moment.'

    Thin, wool-covered hands grabbed her upper arms and shook her. "Hey!" someone cried. "Hey, lady! You gotta get up! You don't wanna freeze out here in the middle of Siberia. My house is just over there. C'mon, you're strong, you can do this..." The words came back to her...her beloved Loki, encouraging her to bring little Narfi into the world.

    "I can't push anymore," she wailed. "Too tired. Just gonna sleep a second...too tired..."

More hands grabbed her… small, icy hands pulled at her arms and shoulders. "Come on, Mummy, you can do it, come on." Her eyes were frozen shut, and she was so tired, but she struggled to stand. She thought her blood must be frozen, because it was hard to move anything. She found herself stumbling forward, moving inches at a time. "I can do this," she mumbled through cracked lips. "Just help me, Loki. We can do this together." She hugged the strangely shrunken and hunched figure of Loki, but no, this wasn't Loki. She was banished, banished to some godforsaken corner of the universe. She had condemned herself and her children to death, trying desperately to save Loki.

And then there was warmth. And light. A warm cloth was placed over her eyes, and they began to thaw enough for her to open them and look around. Her children were wrapped in some kind of furry animal skins, lying in front of a gorgeous, welcoming fire. She looked at her hands, and saw with horror that they were black.

"It's okay, my dear, they'll come back. But it's gonna hurt like hell." The old woman brought a pan of cold water and set it on the table in front of her. "Here. Put your hands in this. Don't want to thaw them out too quickly. Try to wiggle them a little now and then, get your circulation going."

Sigyn noticed that she had stopped shivering while lying on the cold ground. Now, she began to shiver violently. She thought she might break bones, her limbs jerked so hard.

"That's good," said the old woman. "You know you're in trouble when the shivering stops while you're out there. You're gonna be just fine." She brought a mug of hot liquid and took it to Sigyn's lips. "I don't suppose you can hold on to this, yet, but you should try to drink it down. Hot yak's milk. Fix you right up," she concluded. The smell and taste were vile, but at that moment, it was nectar from Valhalla. She savored the warmth as it coursed down her throat and into her belly. She tried to speak, but her throat decided it just wasn't ready yet, and could do no more than squeak. She motioned towards her children, now curled up asleep in front of the fire.

"They're fine, dear. They've had their milk, and their appendages seemed to have fared better than yours. Let them sleep. They've had a bad day." The woman smiled, but Sigyn's split and cracked lips wouldn't allow her to smile in return.

"Thank you," Sigyn rasped. Then her hands began to ache—her sense of feeling was returning. She felt a thousand needles and horrible pressure under her fingernails. She wanted to scream, but knew it was impossible.

"Yes, they're getting blood now. Here, drink this." This time the liquid was familiar. Warm mead and honey. She gulped it down, and tried to think of anything but the unrelenting pain in her fingers. The warmth of the mead soon spread and even seemed to relieve some of the stinging and aching in her hands. "Things will look better in the morning. Go ahead and lie down there in the bed. I'll look after the boys."

Sigyn was asleep as soon as her head hit the pillow.

*   *   *

The next morning, Sigyn opened her eyes. The pain in her hands was gone, and she actually felt warm. But the old woman was wrong. Things did not look better this morning. She was still here, in a hell made of ice. How could she raise two boys in a wasteland like this? What kind of future could they possibly have here? She cursed the gods, her parents, Odin, Thor, Frigga, and even her dearest Loki. She was too miserable to cry. Instead, she just lay there, staring at the spare dirt floor of the lowly little cabin. The boys were awake, helping the old woman drop sliced vegetables into a huge cauldron hanging by the fire. They were actually laughing, and their laughter awoken something in her. A memory, a memory from a hundred years ago, of Loki, Vali, Narfi, and herself in a small bedroom in the kingdom of Scandia. They had all laughed then, hadn't they? And then the tears came. Great wracking sobs that shook her frail body to its core. "I'm so sorry, Vali. So sorry, Narfi. Please, please, forgive me," she sobbed.

The boys rushed to her bed and climbed in, hugging her so tightly, she thought she might not be able to breathe. "Forgive what, Mother?" asked Vali.

"There's nothing to forgive, Mummy," said Narfi. They stroked her hair and wiped her face, holding her until the sobbing ceased. "Mummy," started Narfi, "This lady says she knows you, and that you know her. She said she almost fainted when she found us. She said she thought we were Dad. Her name is Syr. She said she was your teacher."

Sigyn now stared more closely at the old woman, who quietly stirred a delicious smelling stew that was boiling gently in the pot. She didn't remember Syr as being so old, but banishment to such a wasteland might age a person after all, she thought to herself. "Syr?" she asked tentatively.

"Yeah, it's me, honey. Let myself go a little, I know, but who am I gonna try to impress out here? I mean, there's the occasional elk or reindeer, but they never call you in the morning," she chuckled at her own joke. "Here, have a little rabbit stew. I was waiting to try out this recipe for when company dropped by."

Syr handed out bowls of varying sizes and filled each with the bubbling stew. They sat at the little table and broke off chunks of surprisingly fresh bread to dip into their soup. The boys ate hungrily, soon emptying their bowls. They glanced at their mother, as if to get permission to ask for more. Syr chuckled and grabbed their bowls to fill again with the savory pottage.

Sigyn appreciated the food, but she could not bring herself to eat. Her mind was filled with images of the events of the past few days. She worried that Loki might have believed her story of spell casting and now hated her. She worried that he had not believed it and now hated Odin and might do something stupid to avenge her. She worried about Fingardin. Since it was she who was banished, and not he, she feared that the people of Scandia would suffer under his unrestrained hand once more. How had things gone so horribly wrong? She rested her head on her hands and gazed into her food as if to find the answers there.

She felt Syr's boney hand on her shoulder. "There's a way to find out, you know. About the future, I mean."

Sigyn jerked to attention. "What's that? How?"

"The Third Eye," Syr whispered. She then went over to a tall cupboard in the far corner of the room. She shuffled around the bottom shelf, and finally emerged with what looked like a crystal ball with a large crack down the middle. On closer inspection, the crack turned out to be a vertical pupil, like the eye of a cat. "You aim it towards the place you're interested in, then you ask it the question you want answered about the future and hold it up to your forehead. It takes some getting used to, but you'll see the future there." She went to a small front facing window and looked to the north.

"There it is," she said. "Asgard."

Sigyn rushed to her side. "What do you see? Is Loki alright?" She peered into the sky as if to will herself the ability to see Asgard for herself.

Syr allowed her mind to open so that she might "see" through the glass. She saw the immediate future, which is to say, she saw Loki beside himself with grief, begging Heimdall to tell him that his family was safe. She took the ball down; she found it difficult to see her former favorite student so wracked with pain. She quickly brightened, not wanting to worry her guests. "So, what'll it be? Five years? Ten?"

The realization suddenly hit Sigyn that they were going to be here a long, long time, maybe forever. Sigyn swore that she would get them home, somehow. "What realm is this?" she asked.

"This is Midgard, home to the humans. I believe we're about 1,500 miles from the nearest town. But you're lucky. They put you here in the height of summer. In winter it's much colder." Syr told her.

Sigyn pondered Syr's words. "How about tomorrow, Syr? Or now... I want to know if he's alright now."

"Now, eh?" She looked into Sigyn's tortured eyes. "Sure. Why not?" She took some deep breaths and concentrated on the palace of Asgard. She cleared her mind, closed her eyes, and imagined a spot in the palace as it should be at that very moment. She opened her eyes and her mind and gazed at an empty courtyard. She felt as if she were floating above it and willed herself to fly into the castle.

Odin sat at his throne, seemingly in deep conversation with his advisers. Gliding along the sparsely populated corridors, she found the huge open doorway to the Rainbow Bridge. She heard a roar at the entrance to the Bifrost, and was shocked to see Loki screaming at Heimdall, who was standing motionless. Others must have heard the commotion, too, as she saw Thor running towards them, hammer in hand.

Floating down closer, she heard Loki crying *"No, no, no, no, no!* You're lying to me, Heimdall! You're lying!" He then sank to his knees, and slowly collapsed.

Thor crouched next to his brother. "What have you done? Is he dead?" He glared at the guard of Bifrost.

Heimdall glanced impassively down at the unconscious Loki. "He demanded to know the fate of his children and their mother. I told him they were dead. I told him the fire went out in their hut, and they froze to death in their sleep during the night."

"My god, Heimdall, did you tell it to him like that?" Thor picked up Loki's limp body, readying to take him to the healing room.

"What other way is there?" the guard replied.

Loki stirred, and forced himself out of his brother's grasp. He staggered slightly, and then whispered, "They're gone, Thor. They're gone." He gazed at the edge of the Bridge, and with a sudden jolt, took off, wanting to throw himself into the roaring river below.

"Loki, no!" shouted Thor. He ran after him, catching him as his first foot just cleared the edge.

He held Loki close. "I'm so sorry, brother, so sorry."

Syr jerked the ball from her brow. She was incensed. Heimdall had just lied to Loki, told him his family was dead. Why would he do something so cruel? Heimdall was probably Odin's most loyal follower. Could Odin have put him up to this? Sigyn saw the look on the seer's face, and her own turned white.

"What is it? Has something happened to Loki?" Her question was barely audible. Her hands trembled as she laid them on the woman's arm.

"No, well, yes. Heimdall just told him you and the boys died in your sleep last night."

What little blood that was left in Sigyn's face drained away, and her knees buckled beneath her. Syr caught her and helped her to a chair. "So what happened next? Did Loki…" She paused uncertainly. "…move on? Will he find another family? Will he be okay?"

Syr raised the crystal to her brow. She held her right index finger in the air, moving it side to side, as if flipping the pages of a book. Once in a while, she let out a little gasp, or a plaintive, "Oh, no." After some time, she lowered the ball wearily. She laid sad eyes on Sigyn. "Well, there's good news, and bad news. Loki lives, but he becomes sort of damaged, in his mind. There remains some tiny part of him that doesn't believe you're dead and he thinks Odin is hiding information from him. He wants to win the love and trust of his father so he can garner the truth. He has done many favors for Odin, favors that Odin couldn't do himself because they were rather…" She paused. "…unpleasant in nature. And by the way, you're a widow."

Syr sat at a chair near Sigyn, and placed her hands over hers. "Are you sure you want to hear all this, sweetie?" she asked.

She wasn't sure. What she was sure of was that she needed to go to Loki, or at least get some message to him. Her eyes strayed about the room, and then fell upon her boys. Her wonderful, talented boys. "Syr," she began, "Loki was quick to learn, wasn't he? Do you think you could teach Vali and Narfi?"

The old woman smiled into Sig's face. "Yes," she said. "That's a very good idea."

Asgard

Loki spent many years away from his home in Asgard. He mourned the loss of his family and felt betrayed by Odin. Loki also felt the deepest responsibility for the deaths of Sigyn and their sons. His impatience and bad judgment had led to it all. He had thought often of suicide, but his nature pushed him in another direction--revenge. Somehow, he would discredit his brother, seize the throne of Odin, and overthrow Asgard. They would all pay for the wrongs they had inflicted upon him and his family.

While visiting yet again a tavern in the town of Tobolsk, in the realm of Midgard, Loki overheard a conversation between two fur traders, recently returned from an extensive hunting trip further north.

"Good thing you turned back, Yuri. A few more miles, and you might have run into the witch!" he laughed.

"I've heard she's got herself some slaves now. A woman and a couple of boys. Tevi says she'll eat them come winter," replied the one called Yuri.

"Ach, all superstition and paranoia," scoffed the first man. "No one could live there. These are just the stories parents tell their children at night to keep them from wondering off." He gulped down his beer, slamming the mug on the table.

Something about the man's story struck a chord in Loki's chest. A woman and two boys. It couldn't be... Then, he was angry with the man for sparking some ember of hope within his breast. With a slight flick of his wrist, Loki cracked the legs under the man's chair and smiled to himself as it crumbled beneath him. The man saw the smile on Loki's face and flared up at him.

"You find humor in this?" he demanded.

Loki smirked. "No, I find humor in this," flicked his wrist again, and hurled the man through the back wall of the tavern. The other patrons stood and stared in horror at this new threat, this tall, dark stranger. Yuri was first to run out, to check on his friend. The others ran out to protect themselves. Loki left several pieces of gold on the bar. "This should compensate you," he said to the barkeep. "Just having a little fun is all. Sorry for the mess."

Loki was haunted by the notion that his beloved wife and children might still be alive. It would be just like Heimdall to lie to him, just to hurt him. Heimdall had always hated him, although Loki could never understand why. Sure, Loki flaunted authority, and he did love his little joke, but Heimdall's hatred of him seemed extreme. And Loki was, after all, a prince of the House of Odin. Could he have told him such a lie without the command of Odin himself? It was all too impossible. They were gone, and he had to accept it.

Loki finally returned to Asgard. His brother, Thor, greeted him with great hugs and much backslapping and celebration. There was still some affection between them, even though Loki was forever envious of Thor's favor amongst the citizens of Asgard and at court. Thor knew Loki to be by far the greater intellect and admired and respected him. Loki knew Thor had a good heart, but was sure that his quick temper, combined with his amazing, unfettered strength, would make him a terrible leader. Odin had made his decision, however. He had made plans to hand over his throne to Thor very soon.

Loki had a plan of his own. He had to invent some sort of diversion, some sort of spectacular event to disrupt his brother's coronation. He had to let Thor's hotheadedness be his own undoing. All he had to do was make the first move.

Twin Sorcerers

Many years had passed. Syr had taught Narfi and Vali about particles and how to manipulate them. They had mastered transfiguration, and Sigyn was beginning to understand why Odin had banished Syr. The tricks they played were sometimes amusing, but mostly, they were very annoying. They had attempted to conjure up various types of food, but the food was tasteless and empty. They were not the masters their father was, but they were improving each day. Syr had no doubt that their abilities would actually surpass even the powerful Loki one day. They seemed to be able to read each other's minds, as well, and when they concocted a spell together, the results could be mind-boggling.

Sigyn stared at the thin forest of red and purple trees that now surrounded the house. They were the result of one of the boys' joint efforts. The trees had served to block the constant numbing blasts of arctic wind that had once made their lives so miserable. Sigyn still thought of them as boys, but they were rapidly becoming young men. Soon, they would be the same age she and Loki were when they had consummated their love. She missed Loki today as much as the day they last parted, but gazing into her sons eyes, she could see their father and almost had him there with her again.

*   *   *

"Narfi, Vali, we are going to try something new today," began Syr, motioning the two to come sit at the table. "At this point, how far have you transported yourselves?"

"No further than the land we could see, Syr. You told us we might appear inside a mountain or cleaved into a human or animal," offered Vali.

Narfi's eyes turned down as he found something fascinating to stare at on the floor.

"Narfi, is that true? Have you only traveled as far as you could see?" asked Syr.

Narfi turned his soulful eyes on Syr. "Actually, I have gone a bit further," he began. "I have turned myself into an eagle, and flown high enough to see two hundred miles from here. I then transported myself, in eagle form to that spot, still flying."

Syr was astonished. Two forms of magic at once? It was unprecedented. And possibly very dangerous. There were reasons practitioners of magic avoided such spells. "Once you were there, how did you feel?"

"It all felt quite natural," he stated. "I've done it several times, even gone as far as the nearest town."

"That's 1,500 miles away," whispered Sigyn. "How long did it take you?"

"The first trip took longer, maybe three minutes. But once I knew where I was going, it was instantaneous," said Narfi.

Syr was deep in thought. Narfi had traveled 1,500 miles away and back. Asgard was hundreds of thousands of miles away. But distance really should not matter, since one was moving one's particles at the speed of light. She thought they might remember the palace, but possibly not well enough to arrive within it safely. And there could be asteroids, comets between here and Asgard. "I need to think about this," she said, and threw her heavy bear fur coat over her shoulders, and walked outside.

Sigyn had not looked through The Third Eye in many months. The Loki she had seen was colder, harder. She wanted desperately to be with him, before she lost him forever. She needed to see his face again, so she quietly withdrew the crystal from the bottom shelf, and placed it between her eyes. She had done this so many times, the vision came almost immediately. There was the palace, but Loki was not to be seen.

She concentrated now on seeing just him, and as through a cloud, she saw his tall form moving along a rough stone path. As the vision cleared, she saw him in a dark, desolate place. She saw three, large figures in front of him. With a start, Sigyn knew he was in Jotunheim. The figures were giants, and Loki silently waved his hands in front of him, and they disappeared. Loki then vanished, himself. She searched for him, and soon discovered him back at the palace. It was Thor's coronation day. Loki seemed genuinely happy for his brother and smiled as Thor strode triumphantly down the long aisle that led to the platform of Odin's throne.

She watched, her heart aching. Odin was about to pronounce Thor King, when he stopped mid-sentence. "Jotun," he said.

She snatched the crystal from her face. "Oh, Loki, what are you thinking?" she moaned. She was afraid to look further. Loki had brought Jotun into Asgard. Why? What sort of scheme had he cooked up now? Reluctantly, she brought the crystal up to her face again. As the vision appeared, she gently moved her right index finger to the left, moving time ahead just a few hours. Thor, Loki, and four of Thor's friends were in the banquet hall. Thor had ravished the place. From the conversation amongst them, she determined that the Jotun had been summarily vanquished by The Destroyer. Thor had wanted to attack Jotunheim immediately, but Odin had shouted him down and postponed the coronation.

"I agree with you, my brother, but there's nothing you can do, at least not without disobeying Father," said Loki.

The seeds were planted. Thor announced that he would go to Jotunheim and slay as many of the giants he possibly could.

He convinced the rest to join him, and they set out for their quest.

Sigyn skipped forward some more until she saw them fighting the giants of Jotun. She felt her heart would beat itself out of her chest as she saw Loki almost fall off a cliff, only to teleport himself safely behind some rocks. The Frost Giant, unable to stop in time, flew over the cliff instead. She saw the others fight valiantly, until one of the warriors was gravely wounded. Loki's arm was grabbed by one of the giants, but instead of his flesh burning as it would on any other Asgardian, his skin remained unharmed but turned the same blue coloring as the Jotun. After his initial shock, he quickly dispensed with the giant and joined his fellow warriors in a hasty retreat.

Luckily for them, just as the Jotunheim giants who outnumbered them fifty to one were about to descend upon them, Odin appeared and took them via the Bifrost back to Asgard. Looking ahead more rapidly again, Sigyn saw

Thor banished to Earth, stripped of all his powers. Scrolling through the future, she saw Thor undergo a transformation. He learned humility and self-sacrifice. He had, in fact become a man worthy to become King. Odin had fallen into the Odin-sleep, and Loki was pronounced King of Asgard.

"This is all too much," Sigyn sighed.

"What's that?" asked Syr, walking back into the warmth of the little hut.

"I think I've just seen what you've hoped I wouldn't see all these years, Syr. I think I've seen my Loki becoming a cold, ambitious man. Is this the only possible future? If we do finally find our way back, will it even change anything?"

Syr walked over to Sigyn and wrapped her gently in her arms. "I don't know, my dear. But it's worth a try, isn't it? These are all possible outcomes based on what is happening right now, in the present. If we change the now, then it must follow that we change the future, doesn't it? How far did you look, dearie?"

"To the point where Loki became King," she said, her voice so low as to be barely heard.

"Ah," she said. "That's the point that you *must* arrive back in Asgard. It will be the events not long after his taking the throne that will lead to his downward spiral. Thor needs to be banished to Earth. He needs to learn restraint, patience, and humility, if he would become king. Loki doesn't really want the throne. He wants to destroy Jotunheim, because he can't stand that he's part Jotun, and this new power would help him do just that. But if you were there, you could be the strength he needs to cope with all that. He could let go of all the bitterness and hate if only he had those whom he has always loved the most, you and his sons."

"How soon will that be? The boys, they're not ready yet." Sigyn paused, then asked, "Are they?"

"I think I have a solution," Syr smiled. She walked back outside, to where the boys stood, patiently waiting their next lesson. Addressing them, she said, "What you need is a shield. A surrounding force to protect you should you find yourselves transported into a wall, or, the gods forbid, into a living creature. Imagine yourselves surrounded by a cloak, or, better yet, a bubble that is totally impenetrable."

Vali and Narfi closed their eyes, emptying their minds of all thoughts but the conjuring of the shield. Narfi opened his eyes, feeling a warmth that now surrounded him. Vali opened his as well, but instead of warmth, he felt intense heat. His clothes actually started to smoke. Syr shook him to break his concentration before he could burst into flame. "Try again, Vali, but imagine the force is just slightly away from your body. Imagine there's a cushion of air keeping you cool and safe from the energy." He tried again, and this time he was aware of some warmth but remained quite comfortable.

For the next few weeks, the boys practiced their shields, transporting themselves into soft snowdrifts and emerging dry and warm. They tried bales of hay and piles of pillows. Narfi grew tired of appearing within such innocuous barriers, and, without Syr's or his mother's knowledge, attempted to reappear within the trunk of one of the trees that surrounded the house. There was a thunderous crack, and the tree was split in two. Narfi, however, was untouched. Vali tried the same trick but found himself thrown some fifteen feet away from the trunk.

It was obvious to Syr that each boy had great talent. Vali exhibited strength--he was the most able to move heavy objects and explode boulders or bore trenches through the earth with ease. Narfi, however, was by far the better with more subtle magic; his shields and cloaks were impenetrable, and his powers of persuasion were almost impossible to deny. And where Vali usually needed great concentration to perform his more powerful magic, Narfi seemed to be completely relaxed, almost bored, as he did some of the most difficult conjuring Syr had ever seen. For example, the crude shack they had inhabited for so long was now a large and sturdy log chalet. Syr had watched him perform the transition as they all stood outside; he had simply closed his eyes and lifted his hands. As they lifted, so rose the house, with Narfi simply smiling, slowly dropping his head back, with a look of complete happiness and satisfaction across his face.

  While the boys were out practicing one afternoon, Syr sat with Sigyn at the kitchen table, the site of their most intimate conversations. "Sig," she began, "I think Vali should stay here." She noted the look of confusion on Sig's face. "I know I said they should both go, but I don't think Vali is ready.

Not yet, and we're out of time. Somehow, you've got to break it to him. Convince him he must stay. I know he'll be hurt, but..."

Sig covered Syr's hands with her own. "Are you sure that Narfi is ready? Are you asking me to make send only one so that I might not lose them both?"

"Oh no, my dear, I believe that Narfi has been ready for weeks. His talent is very special indeed. He is more adaptable, more able to think on his feet, you see. Vali is very talented, too, but for something like this, I'm afraid he just, well--he just isn't ready."

Sig was thoughtful for some time. "Leave it to me," she said. Standing at the doorway, she called to her firstborn, Vali. Tall and handsome, the young teen turned with a last playful shove to his brother and went inside. "Vali," she began. "Syr tells me she has seen hunters near here in the forest, at night. They are few, as you know. We see them quite rarely. But she senses something..." she paused, "...malevolent, about them. You, my son are the stronger. I beg you, please, stay here with me and Syr while your brother goes to Asgard. Once he has found your father, we shall all go back to Asgard together. But please, my darling, you must be the man here for just a while."

Vali's face fell. He had been training for so long, working so hard. How could his mother ask him this? "But, I need to be with Narfi. We need to go together. That was the plan all along, Mother. Please," he said, his eyes pleading.

"So you would leave us here alone, to fend for ourselves? Vali, I need you here. I would rather that you volunteer, but if you force me to demand it..." Sig let her voice drop. She was ashamed of herself for lying to her son, but she knew the truth would hurt him more. She saw his expression turn sulky as he bowed his head.

"Of course, Mother. As you wish."

With that, he walked, bent, up to his room.

Trip to Asgard

Syr consulted The Eye one last time. She anxiously wrung her hands and paced the room. Narfi and Vali were deep in quiet conversation in one corner. "It's time," she announced. The boys thumped each other's fists together, and Narfi slapped his hand behind Vali's neck. "I wish you were going with me," he said.

Vali glanced at his mother. "You and me both, brother." His head drooped. "Just come back quickly, and bring Father with you," he whispered.

"Of course. Take care of Mum and Syr, will you?" Narfi felt his brother's pain. He would truly miss his company, but, in his heart, he felt the decision for only him to go was a wise one.

They all went outside and stood in front of the house, faces to the north. Sig approached

Narfi, a small bundle in her hands. "Narfi, your father gave this to me the first night we were parted. It's a sleeve from his shirt. I've always kept it round my waist or neck, so that I may feel that he is still with me. If he has any doubts, show him this. Please be careful, my child. If things go badly for some reason, come home. Come home safely to me." She hugged him to her breast and kissed his face all over.

"Mum, I'll be fine, really. There's nothing to worry about. We've gone over everything a hundred times. What could go wrong?" Narfi grinned at his mother. He knew of dozens of things that could go wrong, but he didn't want to see his mother fret.

Syr took them to the spot with the best view of the northern sky. She took Narfi's hands into hers and said, "I know you can do this, Narfi. Remember the palace. Remember The Bridge. Concentrate on the Bridge. Place yourself about fifteen feet above its surface. Do you remember how your father dressed?" she asked.

Puzzled, Narfi replied, "Yes, I think so."

"Then conjure up a similar outfit for yourself. You don't want to attract attention. Try to look like any other Asgardian." She noticed just a slight jerk of Narfi's hand, and he was suddenly wearing his father's uniform, complete with helmet. "Loose the headgear, dear. Don't draw attention, remember?"

In a flash, the helmet was gone. Sig felt her heart leap into her throat, seeing her son now looking even more like his father. She embraced him one last time as he turned, facing upwards and to the north.

"Well, see you soon," he said. Then he closed his eyes and vanished.

* * *

Narfi felt that he hadn't traveled more than a second, when he felt himself stop. He opened his eyes and saw that he was hovering above The Rainbow Bridge. It was night, and the Bifrost was deserted. He was no more than ten feet from the entrance to the palace and began walking towards it. He was flooded with memories. The grandeur of the palace, all the pomp and ceremony of meeting the King for the first time, and then the memory of the banishment, his father's screams, the rough hands of the guards.

He immediately made himself invisible. Even though he was still shielded, he really didn't want to confront any palace guards right now. He walked deeper into the palace, hoping to find his father, the new King, at his throne. The seat was empty. Now, he wasn't sure what to do. A servant entered from somewhere to the right and picked up an empty goblet that had been sitting on an arm of the throne. Narfi decided to follow this servant, hoping to overhear a conversation that would lead him to Loki.

His intuition paid off. The servant met another in the kitchen. "He's in a mood tonight, Dor. Drank down his mead and just marched off to the upper deck. Just stares out over the Bifrost, he does. Misses his brother, I dare say."

Narfi remembered a stairway that seemed to wind upwards from the passage to the kitchen. He doubled back, and climbed the stairs. Trembling, he turned the corner to step out onto the huge deck that looked over all of Asgard. There, at the edge, stood a tall, dark man. Narfi approached cautiously, felt himself become visible again, and as the shield dropped, he spoke. "Hello, Father."

Loki whipped himself around to face this madman who had penetrated his defenses. He pointed his spear directly at the intruder's heart. Then he stood motionless, staring. Loki had been deceived before, and this could be the cruelest deceit of all. "How dare you?" he demanded. "How did you get in here?"

Narfi raised his hands and spoke, "It really is me, father. It's Narfi. And I have something for you, from Mother." He drew the tattered green sleeve from his jacket. "She said you gave it to her, to remind her of you," he finished, offering him the sleeve with outstretched hand

Loki's eyes rested on the worn piece of material and thought for a moment that he had surely died. This could not be his son standing in front of him. It had to be another lie or some elaborate illusion. He looked into his son's eyes, and, at that instant, he didn't care. He wanted more than anything to believe. He ran across the deck and embraced his son. He tried to speak, but all he managed was, "How?"

"It's simple. I'm Loki's son." came the reply.

Loki grinned as he hugged his son more tightly. "You're not dead. You're truly and honestly alive, and you're here! Narfi, my boy, my son!" shouted Loki.

Narfi stood back from his father, an earnest look upon his face. "Father, Dad, what you've done, what you've been doing, you need to stop," he said. "You need to bring Thor back. He's changed, really. And you mustn't destroy Jotunheim. You don't have to prove yourself to your father. You don't have to prove yourself to anyone. Please, Dad, come with me to Earth. Let's go get Mum and Vali, please?" he begged.

Loki's back straightened as he looked down at the boy. This was sounding more like a trick, but he was inclined to go along with it. With Odin's staff and the casket of Jotunheim, he knew he had the power to deflect any attack. Besides, his plans could wait a day. With a little doubt in his voice, he said, "All right, let's go to your mother. We can take the Bifrost, but I doubt Heimdall will be of any help. You'll have to lead the way,"

Narfi heard the doubt in his father's voice but was happy he was still going to travel back to Earth with him. They strode down the Bifrost and came to Heimdall. Narfi could feel the hatred emanating from this man and took an instant dislike to him. "Let us pass," Loki demanded.

With what seemed minutes of hesitation, the guard of Bifrost allowed his King and his son to pass. "What is your destination, my lord?" he asked.

"That's the business of me and my son. Now present, so that we may be on our way," Loki commanded.

Again, after much hesitation, Heimdall placed his sword into the key, and Loki and Narfi were swept away.

Reunion

    Loki and Narfi landed with a crack just outside the front door of the chalet. Loki reached for the handle, but suddenly it was thrown open, his beloved Sig standing in the light of the doorway. He stared down at her, unable to believe his eyes. She threw her arms around him, and he smothered her with his. Their kiss was long, hungry, and deep. Finally, they broke apart, and Vali rushed into his father's arms, as well. Syr stood quietly, her hand over her mouth as if to keep her grin from splitting her face, while tears rolled down her cheeks.

    Many hugs and tears later, the family gathered around the kitchen table. Loki sat between his sons opposite Sig, with Syr at the head. "I should never have believed them," Loki began. "I should have looked for you..." His voice trailed off.

"It's alright, Father," stated Vali. "We've done alright. It's not your fault. Odin cloaked us, anyway. You'd have never found us."

"It's routine. Asgard law states that the banished should be cloaked just so no one may find them again. And if Thor hadn't sent us to Syr, we..." said Narfi.

"Thor? Sent you to Syr?" Loki was astonished. His brother had arranged for his family to be sent to Syr? How?

Syr answered, "I saw it, with The Third Eye. He could not stop Odin's command from being carried out, but he could have some influence with Heimdall. Heimdall could not refuse such a request from the son of Odin. Thor had no idea where I was, of course, so he simply commanded that Heimdall set them all down with me, as close as possible. I couldn't believe it when these two small boys, replicas of you at that age, came beating on my door to come save their mother."

Loki rested his head in his hands. Barely audible, he responded, "What you have suffered, the years we have all lost. They must pay for this. Odin, and the rest of those pompous, arrogant Asgardians, must pay for this!" He dropped his hands to the table, eyes hard.

Sig placed her hands over her husband's. "Loki, no. It's over. Revenge serves no one. It only makes things worse. Please, let's just go home and live the lives we were destined to lead."

Loki sat back and stared at his wife. His heart had been hardened by years of rejection and hatred from the citizens of Asgard, as well as the look of apparent disappointment he saw whenever he looked into his father's eyes. He might have committed more than his share of mischief, but he had always made things right, even made things better for all involved. Loki's shoulders then relaxed, as he broke into a wide smile. "Revenge? Never revenge, my love. All

I want is to maintain a sort of balance. I'm thinking of some sort of little prank to play, one that will give them pause for thought, that's all."

He patted his wife's hand. "But for now, we must go to Thor. I've a lot of explaining to do to my brother," he added.

Sig's smile was guarded. Loki was no longer the naive adolescent. He was a man grown cold by the harsh circumstances of his life. She only hoped his roles as father and husband would warm his heart once more.

The party followed Loki outside. Loki scanned the sky, his eyes settling on a spot almost due east of the chalet. Sig stood in front of him, placing a hand on his cheek. His eyes softened as he gazed into hers. "I never stopped loving you, you know?" he said quietly.

"Nor I, you," she whispered back. "I love you, no other, ever and forever. Come back to us soon, my Loki. Come back, so we may all go home."

He kissed her tenderly, and they dropped their embrace. Loki looked again to the east, and was gone.

Arizona

When Loki saw Thor last from his throne in Asgard, Thor had been reunited with Mjolnir. It was at that moment that Narfi had reached him on the palace deck. He wasn't sure, then, what he might find when he entered the small Arizona town. He stood at one end of what had to have been the main street of the town and looked out over the chaos wrought by the Destroyer he had sent. He smiled inwardly, thinking that such mayhem was usually done by his hand. Through rapidly dissipating smoke, he saw a party of people surrounding a tall, red caped figure. As an extra effort at caution, Loki conjured Odin's spear and his own horned helmet. After his recent actions, he was sure that he was not going to be welcomed here.

A woman standing next to the tall figure of Thor saw him first, her mouth agape. The rest turned to look and all gazed at Loki, as he strode down the middle of the wreckage. Their faces turned from looks of surprise to that of rage.

Loki stopped and stood still, arms at his side. "I do not come to fight, brother," he called out.

"Loki, you sent The Destroyer to kill us all. Why shouldn't I kill you where you stand?" demanded Thor.

"A valid question," Loki said. "Circumstances have changed. Some information has come to light that indicates that certain truths have been kept from me, that certain lies have been told to me. I have only been acting as I have as a result of those deceits. I must admit, that as the Master of Deception, I'm a little chagrined at having not seen it." Loki now stood within his brother's reach. "I also understand that you had no part in these deceits, and that when you had the chance, you tried to do what you could to save my family.

Please, forgive me, brother. I swear, I had no idea." And with that, he held out his hand.

Thor stared down at Loki's hand. Sif, standing next to him warned, "Be careful, Thor; this could be another trick."

One of the humans of the party, a woman named Ann, stood at Thor's other side. "He looks sincere," she said. "I mean, wouldn't he have done something already, from over there, where he had better advantage?" She then held out her own hand. "Ann Deacon. Glad to meet you, um, Loki, is it?"

Loki took her hand and raised her fingertips to his lips. "It is an honor, Ann Deacon. My brother exhibits good taste," he smiled. Again, he offered his hand to Thor. "Brother?"

After only a moment's hesitation, Thor grasped Loki's hand and then pulled him to his chest, embracing him tightly. Releasing him and then slapping him on the back, he replied, "Of course I forgive you, my brother. I have always felt nothing but love for you, Loki. I never wanted to see you or your family harmed. I am so sorry for all that's happened. But the lies you told me? That Father was dead, that Mother had refused my return, why?"

Loki lost himself in thought for a moment, and then replied, "I needed you out of the way for a while. I needed to sneak Laufey into Odin's bedchamber so that I could slay him, and take credit for saving Odin, and then have sufficient grounds to destroy Jotunheim."

All fell silent. Thor was shocked at his brother's candor and disturbed by the madness of his plan. The jaws dropped on the rest of the party as they stared in astonishment. Thor was first to speak. "Loki, that's a terrible plan. You were seriously going to try to destroy Jotunheim? And put father's life in peril in order to do it? Are you mad?"

Loki smiled jovially. "Actually, yes, I was. I suppose I am still, a bit. I must be mad to reveal all this to you and our friends--well, your friends, I suppose," he said. "But, none of it matters anymore. I never meant for you to be banished, Thor. But when Father fell into the Odin-sleep, and Mother offered me the throne, your absence was, well, convenient. I never wanted to be King, brother. I only ever wanted to be your equal." Loki paused and looked to the west. "And now, I must ask you to join me, to travel to a chalet in Siberia. I would like you to get acquainted with your nephews. They're quite grown now."

Thor was astounded. "My nephews? You don't mean Vali and Narfi? They said they were... That they..." He looked thoughtful and then, a great realization came over him. "The lies, the deceit. Your family didn't die. Heimdall lied to you, and Father concealed the truth as well. Is Sigyn alive as well? Did they find Syr?"

"Yes, thanks to you. Syr took good care of them and trained my sons so that one day they would come to me, and we could at last be rejoined. You saved their lives, Thor. You saved me, as well." Loki placed his hand on Thor's shoulder. Loki grinned, and giving Thor's shoulder a shove, remarked, "That's a blush there, isn't it? You know, I think it's almost all been worth it just to see the Mighty Thor blush!"

Thor laughed back. "That's no blush, brother! That's the flush of anticipation! I see a great celebration ahead of us! A grand wedding between my brother and his beautiful Sigyn, at long last!" He clapped Loki's back as they strode towards the edge of town.

"Perhaps, after your coronation, you could grant Sig her annulment from Fingarden, and, then, there can *be* a wedding," said Loki.

"Loki, I thought you knew. Fingarden's dead. Has been, for years. Father never...Thor's eyes were troubled. He suddenly realized that with the death of Fingarden, Sigyn's banishment was no longer necessary. Had Loki known, he would have demanded the right to search for her, and if found alive, that they be returned. Odin had deliberately kept this from Loki, had deliberately left Loki's family in a frozen wasteland in Siberia. Somehow, Odin's actions had orchestrated all of this. Loki had been driven to the brink of madness for some purpose known only to Odin.

The brothers exchanged looks. It was clear to Thor that Loki had come to the same conclusion. They both knew their father had bargained for the gift of foresight. They knew that he had looked far into the future, even to Ragnarok, the end of all life.

"Come on then, brother. Time for us to go change the future," said Loki. Thor nodded, and went back to talk with his friends. Ann Deacon and company loaded up the Asgardians to give them a lift to their launching spot back across the Bifrost. Thor and Ann exchanged a kiss, with the promise of reconciliation soon.

Loki said to Thor, "I'll send you on first, then. I'll be right behind." With that, he closed his eyes, and Thor was gone. After a moment, Loki saw his family's chalet in his mind, and in an instant, vanished. He reappeared next to Thor, just outside the front door of Syr's original crude hut. It would be winter soon, and the wind was bone chilling. They entered into the warmth and dim light to find the family sitting around the table, playing a game of cards. They stood up almost as one, and Thor stomped over to greet his nephews.

"By the gods, Loki, where are those boys you spoke of? All I see here are men! Men who, unfortunately, took after their father. Sigyn, I certainly hope they have inherited your wit," he laughed.

First Vali and Narfi greeted their uncle with hugs, and were followed by Sig and Syr. Narfi apologized for changing the chalet back into the hut. "It was a bit taxing, keeping up the spell," he explained. "And since we were leaving anyway, I didn't see the point." His hair was ruffled playfully by Thor, and the group went outside.

Loki removed what appeared to be a toothpick from his pocket. With a wiggle of his wrist, it grew into Odin's spear. He implored the group to gather close, and, with a rap of the spear against the ground, they were all transported via the Bifrost to the Rainbow Bridge.

The New Asgard

Loki, now dressed in full regalia, including cape and golden horned helmet, led the party down the Rainbow Bridge towards the palace entrance. As he passed the guards that stood lining the grand hallway that led to the throne room, he commanded, "Notify the elders and high citizens of Asgard to assemble at court now. Their King has a few announcements to make." Half the guards left immediately to do their King's bidding.

Thor gave his brother a wry smile and said, pressing his arm across his chest, "My King," and gave a small bow.

"Your turn soon enough," replied Loki. "Let me have my bit of fun while I can." The family ascended the steps to the throne, and Loki took his seat of power. The Great Hall filled with the lords and ladies of Asgard, none of whom looked too thrilled to have been summoned by Loki. Murmurs were heard throughout the crowd, as they caught sight of Thor. A few even recognized Sigyn, but were astonished by the sight of the twins, now young men. Syr stood a few paces back, and unnoticed to all, had undergone a transformation. Now back on Asgardian soil, Syr's youth had returned to her. She stood tall, and smiled at the assembly.

"Citizens of Asgard," Loki began. "I hereby rescind the banishment of Sigyn and her sons, Vali and Narfi. I also rescind the banishment of Thor and the sorceress Syr. It is also my proclamation that the unholy union of Fingarden and Sigyn, as it was never consummated, is hereby annulled, and that Sigyn is to be my wife, your Queen, and our sons are true heirs to the throne." Loki stood, glaring at the crowd. Unhappy though they were, no one dare speak out against the King of Asgard.

Loki turned to look at his brother, who was looking at his feet. As a crooked smile crept across Loki's face, he raised his voice again. "And last, it is my wish to leave this throne, and pass the mantle and all the responsibilities therein to the rightful King of Asgard, my brother, Thor Odinson."

After a loud gasp from the assembly, all began to cheer. Thor smiled at his brother, who was holding the Spear of Odin in front of him, to pass it on to the new King. As they now stood face to face, Thor said, "So unexpected, my brother! And so unceremonious!

Loki leaned back, withholding the Spear. "Well, if you'd rather not..."

"No, far be it for me to defy a command from my King." Thor took the Spear, and clapped Loki on his back. "You were a pretty good King, after all," he quipped.

"Better than you'll ever be," Loki replied. "But the paperwork was staggering! Better you than me, brother!"

* * *

Thor dismissed the assembly, and the family, with Syr, walked to Odin's chambers, where he was still immersed in the Odin-sleep. Frigga, ever vigilant by her husband's side, arose and threw her arms around her sons, then Sigyn and the twins. "Loki, I knew you would return your brother to Asgard. And what miracle is this, that you have brought Sigyn and my grandchildren back from the dead?"

"So he deceived even you, Frigga," said Syr, in a harsh, low voice.

A slight stirring occurred from Odin's bed. His eyes opened, and his armor began to assemble itself around him. The blankets disappeared, as did the massive bed, and Odin was left standing in the middle of his room. His countenance was no longer haggard, and his back, no longer bent with weariness. His one eye gazed at only one person in the room--the sorceress, Syr. "Syr," Odin said, "you of all people, should know the necessity of such deception."

"Odin, I, of all people, know no such thing! You're wrong, Odin. You sacrificed one eye to the Norns so that you may have all knowledge of the future. Did you know how we laughed at your foolish gesture? We knew that from then on, you could see only one path into the future. There is no one path, Odin. If you have to manipulate today's events to force your future to occur, then yours is an incorrect future." The Norn Syr had become quite beautiful, her thick black hair gently blowing about her by some invisible breeze.

"You are deluded, dear Syr. There is but the one path, and we are doomed to travel down it, no matter how we try to change it. The Fates have ordained it..." He was stopped by a howl from Syr.

"Fool! I, too, have seen the future, and it is nothing like the one you profess! Look again,

Odin. Sigyn and I have already put the wheels in motion that have diverted the path of your miserable future!" Syr pointed directly at Odin's eye and Odin stood, transfixed, by the visions that appeared in his mind. Peace prevailed throughout the nine realms. Loki remained Thor's greatest counsel and ally, and was never banished again, though thanks to some of his and his sons' pranks, they wisely took a few, long vacations abroad. He looked further and Yggdrasil remained vital and unburned. He saw no evidence of Ragnarok ever occurring. He stumbled and brought himself back to the present.

Syr lowered her hand. "That future may change in time as well, Odin Allfather. The future can only follow the path we draw now. We are all the architects of our own destiny. Now stop meddling in these boys' lives, and let them live them on their own!" A white light surrounded Syr. The light was almost blinding and then began to fade away. Syr faded with it. Her voice, as if from a deep cave, spoke to her students, Thor, Sigyn, and Loki, "Your lives belong to you and no other, my children. Live them well." With that, she was gone.

Thor looked at the Spear in his hands and presented it to his father. Odin looked down at it absently, as though not even sure what the object was. Then, a smile crossed his face as he said, "No, my son. Your King passed this on to you. You are the rightful King of Asgard, now. You're ready. Rule her wisely," he added, with a hand to Thor's shoulder.

"Only with you here to help me, father," replied Thor, his hand covering Odin's.

Loki took Sig's fingers to his lips. "You will marry me, won't you?" he asked with his half smile.

Sig seemed thoughtful. "Well, I don't know. I've been single for so very long now, you know," she teased. Loki took her into his arms and kissed her passionately. Coming up for air, Sig said, "Well, if you put it that way…" and they kissed again.

Epilogue

The Palace Of Asgard was a wonderful place for two curious adolescents to explore. A stairway here might lead to a room full of screeching ghosts. Another, to an armory, where they could don shields and helmets, clashing bright swords, metal against metal. Still another, to a roomful of stars and planets.

One evening, they found a wide stairway leading down, twisting here and there, and getting narrower each step. Eventually, they came to a doorway that opened into a large room divided by a small stream or moat. They thought they saw faces as they stared into the water. There was no way to pass over the wide stream of water, so they conjured a stone bridge, and crossed. Once on the other side, they encountered a large, heavy door.

They tried spell after spell, but could not get the heavy wooden door to give so much as an inch. "I guess that's it," said Vali. "Let's turn back."

Narfi gave the problem more thought. They could not splinter the wood, nor cut any sort of opening through it. He felt along its edges, and found them tight and secure. Then he looked down towards his feet. He saw a faint light reflecting on his boots. "There's a space there," he began. "Watch this," he said, turning himself into a cockroach. He crawled beneath the door with ease and shifted himself whole again. His brother followed just behind and stood next to him again.

Their eyes were drawn to a deep blue cube resting on its own stand near the end of a long corridor lined with open cells. Each cell held some ancient relic of great power and importance to the history of Asgard. But the blue cube was by far the most enticing. It was glowing from within, a swirling cloud of energy flowing inside. The boys ran to it, but the race was a tie. They each took one of the golden handles attached to the side of the cube, and felt its energy glide up their arms. To their astonishment, their arms began to turn blue, the blue coloring rising up into their faces...

The End.

CPSIA information can be obtained at www.ICGtesting.com
Printed in the USA
BVOW012336010513

319672BV00015B/368/P